3 Beloved Tales

# Little RED RIDING HOOD

## Stories Around the World

by Jessica Gunderson

raintree 🍃
a Capstone company — publishers for children

# What is a fairy tale?

Once upon a time, before the age of books, people gathered to tell stories. They told tales of fairies and magic, princes and witches. Ideas of love, jealousy, kindness and luck filled the stories. Some provided lessons. Others simply entertained. Most did both! These fairy tales passed from neighbour to neighbour, village to village, land to land. As the stories spun across seas and over mountains, details changed to fit each culture. A poisoned slipper became a poisoned ring. A king became a sultan. A wolf became a tiger.

Over time, fairy tales were collected and written down. Around the world today, people of all ages love to read or listen to these timeless stories. For many years to come, fairy tales will continue to live happily ever after in our imaginations.

# Little Red Riding Hood
## A German fairy tale

illustrated by
Colleen Madden

Once upon a time, there lived a sweet
girl called Little Red Riding Hood. She got
her name from the red velvet riding hood
she wore. It was a gift from her
adoring grandmother.

One day the girl's mother
gave her a loaf of bread and a
bottle of wine. She said, "Take
these to your grandmother.
She is ill and weak. And
don't stray from the path."

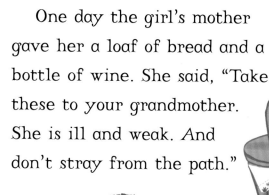

3

Little Red Riding Hood set off through the woods. Along the way, she met a wolf. She didn't know he was a wicked beast, so she wasn't afraid.

"What are you carrying in that basket?" the wolf asked.

"Bread and wine for my grandmother," the girl answered.

"Where does she live?" asked the wolf.

"In a cottage under three big oak trees," said the girl.

The wolf grinned. *She is a tender young thing,* he thought. *She will taste better than the old grandmother. I must be crafty...*

The wolf walked alongside Little Red Riding Hood for a while. Then he said, "Let's race to your grandmother's house and see who gets there first! I'll go this way, and you cut through the trees."

"What a good idea!" the girl exclaimed. She left the path and ran into the woods.

The wolf reached Grandmother's house first and knocked on the door. "It's Little Red Riding Hood," he said in a sweet voice.

"Come in, dear," said Grandmother.

The wolf opened the door and swallowed the poor old woman. He put on her spare cap, nightgown and glasses and got into bed to wait.

Little Red Riding Hood soon arrived. She called, "Hello!" and pulled back the bed covers. The girl thought her grandmother looked very strange. "Grandmother, what big ears you have!" she said.

"The better to hear you with," said the wolf.

"What big eyes you have!" she exclaimed.

"The better to see you with."

"What big hands you have!"

"The better to hug you with."

"Grandmother, what big teeth you have!" Little Red Riding Hood cried.

"The better to eat you with!" the wolf snarled. He jumped out of bed and swallowed the poor girl.

8

Now the wolf felt full. He lay down on the bed and began to snore very loudly.

A hunter passed by and heard the wolf's snores. He saw the wolf on the bed.

He knew the wolf must have eaten the grandmother, so
he grabbed a pair of shears and cut open the wolf's belly.
Out jumped Little Red Riding Hood and her grandmother.

Little Red Riding Hood ran outside and fetched some large stones. She and the hunter filled the wolf's belly with them. When the wolf woke up, he tried to run off. But the stones were so heavy, he fell down dead. The hunter skinned the wolf and took the pelt home with him.

Grandmother ate the bread and drank the wine Little Red Riding Hood had brought and felt better. Little Red Riding Hood told herself she'd never again stray from the path in the woods.

# The False Grandmother
## An Italian fairy tale

illustrated by Eva Montanari

One day a mother was making bread. She told her little girl to run to her grandmother's house and borrow the flour sieve. The girl packed a snack of ring-shaped cakes and bread with oil. Then she set out.

When she reached the river, she asked, "River, will you let me cross?"

The river liked to spin ring-shaped cakes in his whirlpools. He answered, "Yes, if you give me your cakes."

The girl threw the cakes into the river, and the river let her cross.

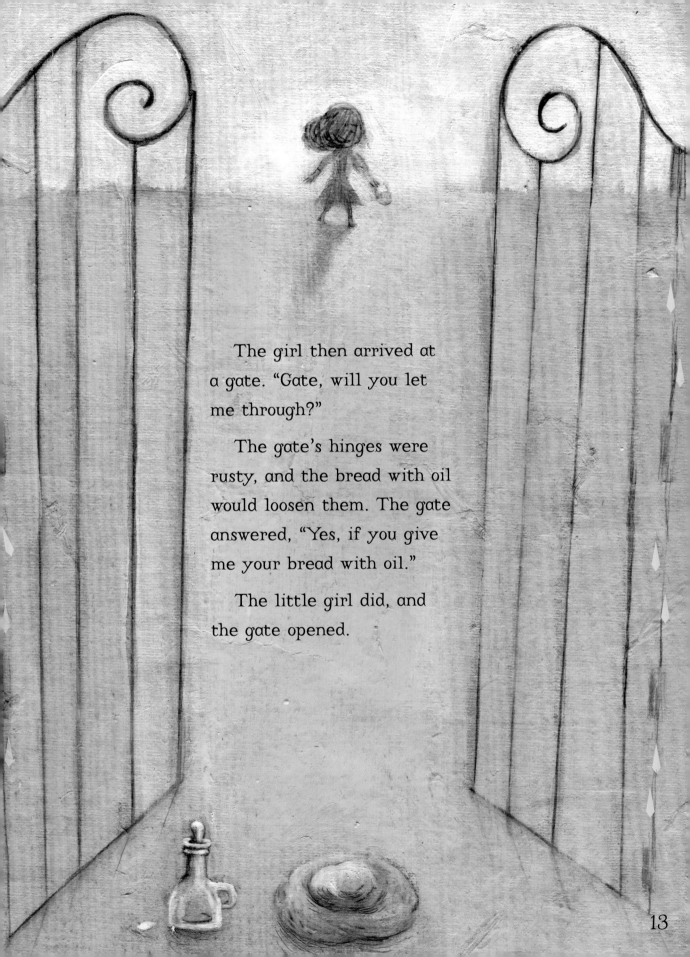

The girl then arrived at a gate. "Gate, will you let me through?"

The gate's hinges were rusty, and the bread with oil would loosen them. The gate answered, "Yes, if you give me your bread with oil."

The little girl did, and the gate opened.

When the girl reached her grandmother's house, she found the door locked. "Grandmother, let me in!" she called.

"I'm sick in bed," Grandmother said. "I'll pull you up through the window." She lowered a rope so the girl could climb up.

The room was dark. The girl couldn't see that in the bed lay an ogress, not her grandmother. The ogress had gobbled up the grandmother.

"Mother wants the sieve," the girl said.

"It's too late. Come to bed now," the ogress said. "I'll give you the sieve tomorrow."

The little girl crawled into bed beside the ogress. "Grandmother, why are your hands so hairy?" she asked.

"From wearing too many rings," the ogress answered.

"Why is your chest so hairy?"

"From wearing too many necklaces."

"Why are your hips so hairy?"

"From wearing my corset too tight."

Then the little girl felt the ogress' tail. She knew her grandmother, hairy or not, had never had a tail. At once she realized the woman was an ogress.

"Grandmother, I have to go to the toilet," the girl said.

"Go to the barn below," said the ogress. She tied a rope around the girl and let her down through the trapdoor.

The moment the girl reached the ground, she untied the rope. She re-tied it around a heavy nanny goat.

"OK! Pull me back up," she called and then ran away.

The ogress pulled and pulled. Up came the nanny goat! The ogress jumped out of bed and chased after the little girl.

The girl reached the gate with the ogress at her heels.
"Don't let her through, Gate!" the ogress yelled.

"Of course I'll let her through," the gate answered.
"She gave me bread with oil."

When the girl reached the river, the ogress yelled, "River, don't let her cross!"

"Of course I'll let her cross," the river answered. "She gave me ring-shaped cakes."

When the ogress tried to cross the river, the waters rose quickly. The ogress was swept away by the current. The little girl stood on the riverbank, making faces at the ogress.

# Grand-aunt Tiger

## A Taiwanese fairy tale   illustrated by Carolina Farias

One day a mother went on an errand and left her two daughters at home alone. She warned them not to open the door to anyone. "Especially not to Grand-aunt Tiger," she said, "the oldest and scariest tiger in the land."

On her way, the mother met an old woman who was very hungry. She gave the old woman all the food she had. But the old woman was still hungry and wanted to eat her hand. The mother didn't know the old woman was really Grand-aunt Tiger in disguise. So she offered her hand. The tiger swallowed it and continued on.

Grand-aunt Tiger now knew the mother's two girls were at home alone. She went to their house. "Open the door!" she called.

The younger sister thought their mother had returned. But the older one said, "Mother's voice is like a bell. This voice is hoarse. It is certainly not Mother."

Grand-aunt Tiger left and went into the mountains. There she drank spring water to rinse her throat. She returned to the house and again called the girls to open the door.

The older sister was still cautious. "Stick your hand inside," she said. She felt the tiger's hand. "Mother's hand is not so coarse."

Grand-aunt Tiger went into the field. She wrapped a potato leaf around her hand. She returned to the house and again stuck her hand inside. The girls felt the soft hand. This time they let her in.

"Mother's face does not have so many moles," the older sister said.

"I'm your mother's mother," the old woman said. The girls had never met their grandmother before, so they believed her. They let her sleep with them.

In the middle of the night, the older sister woke up. She heard the grandmother chewing. "I'm hungry too," she said. "What are you eating?"

"A peanut," the old woman lied. She was really chewing on the younger sister's hand. "Here, take one."

When the girl put the finger to her mouth, she knew it was not a peanut. She realized her grandmother was Grand-aunt Tiger in disguise.

"I have to go to the toilet," the girl said.

"It's dark outside. I'll tie a rope around you so you don't get lost," the old woman said.

The girl scurried outside, untied the rope and re-tied it to a water bucket. When the girl didn't return, the old woman pulled the rope. In came the bucket. Furious, she ran outside, but she couldn't find the girl.

As the sun rose, the old woman saw the girl's shadow. "Come down!" she ordered.

"I know you want to eat me, Grandmother," the girl said. "I will let you. But first I want to eat some fried birds. Will you bring me some boiling oil?"

The old woman agreed. She brought out a wok filled with hot oil and a rope so the girl could pull it up. The girl fried some birds and then said, "OK. I'm ready. Open your mouth, and I will jump in!"

The old woman closed her eyes and opened her mouth. The girl quickly poured the scalding oil into it. Immediately the old woman turned into Grand-aunt Tiger and died.

# Glossary

**corset** woman's tight, stiff undergarment worn to support or give shape to waist and hips

**culture** people's way of life, ideas, art, customs and traditions

**ogress** female monster or giant that eats people; the male version is called an ogre

**pelt** animal's skin with the fur still on it

**sieve** device used to get rid of lumps from a substance such as flour

**wok** cooking pan used for stir-frying food

## Comprehension questions

Find unique cultural elements of each story. How do these elements fit each culture or country?

Compare and contrast the three villains (the wolf, the ogress and the tiger). How are they alike in each of the stories? How are they different?

The Little Red Riding Hood character makes choices in each of the stories. How do these choices affect what happens in each story?

## Writing prompts

1)  Write a Little Red Riding Hood story set where you live. Use details that help identify the place and time of the story (e.g., roads, parks, shops or buildings, people, clothing).

2)  Choose one of the three stories and rewrite it from the point of view of one of the characters. For example, tell Little Red Riding Hood's story as if you were the wolf.

# Read more

Grimm's Fairy Tales (Usborne Illustrated), retold by Ruth Brocklehurst & Gillian Doherty (Usborne Publishing Ltd, 2011)

Little Red Riding Duck (Animal Fairy Tales), Charlotte Guillain (Raintree, 2013)

Why the Spider has Long Legs: An African Folk Tale (Folk Tales from Around the World), Charlotte Guillain (Raintree, 2014)

# Website

www.booktrust.org.uk/books/children/illustrators/illustrations-in-search-of-a-story/

Make your own book with Chris Riddell!

Raintree is an imprint of Capstone Global Library Limited, a company incorporated in England and Wales having its registered office at 264 Banbury Road, Oxford, OX2 7DY – Registered company number: 6695582

www.raintree.co.uk
myorders@raintree.co.uk

Editor: Jill Kalz
Designer: Ashlee Suker
Art Director: Nathan Gassman
Production Specialist: Katy LaVigne
The illustrations in this book were created digitally.

Printed in China
ISBN 978 1 4747 2419 7
20  19  18  17  16
10 9 8 7 6 5 4 3 2 1

British Library Cataloguing in Publication Data
A full catalogue record for this book is available from the British Library.

**Acknowledgements**
Thanks to our advisers for their expertise and advice:

Maria Tatar, PhD, Chair, Program in Folklore & Mythology
John L. Loeb Professor of Germanic Languages & Literatures and Folklore & Mythology, Harvard University

Terry Flaherty, PhD, Professor of English
Minnesota State University, Mankato

Every effort has been made to contact copyright holders of material reproduced in this book. Any omissions will be rectified in subsequent printings if notice is given to the publisher.

All the Internet addresses (URLs) given in this book were valid at the time of going to press. However, due to the dynamic nature of the Internet, some addresses may have changed, or sites may have changed or ceased to exist since publication. While the author and publisher regret any inconvenience this may cause readers, no responsibility for any such changes can be accepted by either the author or the publisher.

# Look out for all the books in this series:

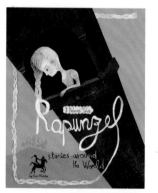